BEAR IN A SQUARE

Written by Stella Blackstone
Illustrated by Debbie Harter

Barefoot Books
Celebrating Art and Story

www.barefootbooks.com

Find the bear in the square

Find the hearts in the queen's hair

Find the circles in the pool

Find the rectangles in the school

Find the moons in the cave

Find the triangles on the wave

Find the diamonds on the crown

Find the zigzags around the clown

Find the ovals in the park

Find the stars
in the dark

Square

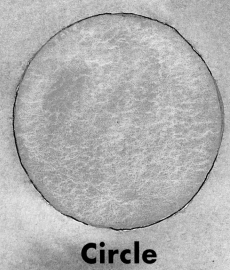

Circle

Heart

Moon

Rectangle

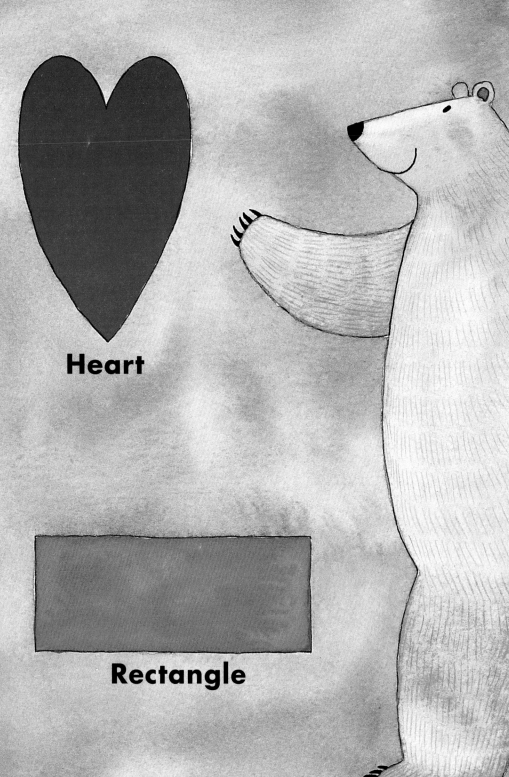

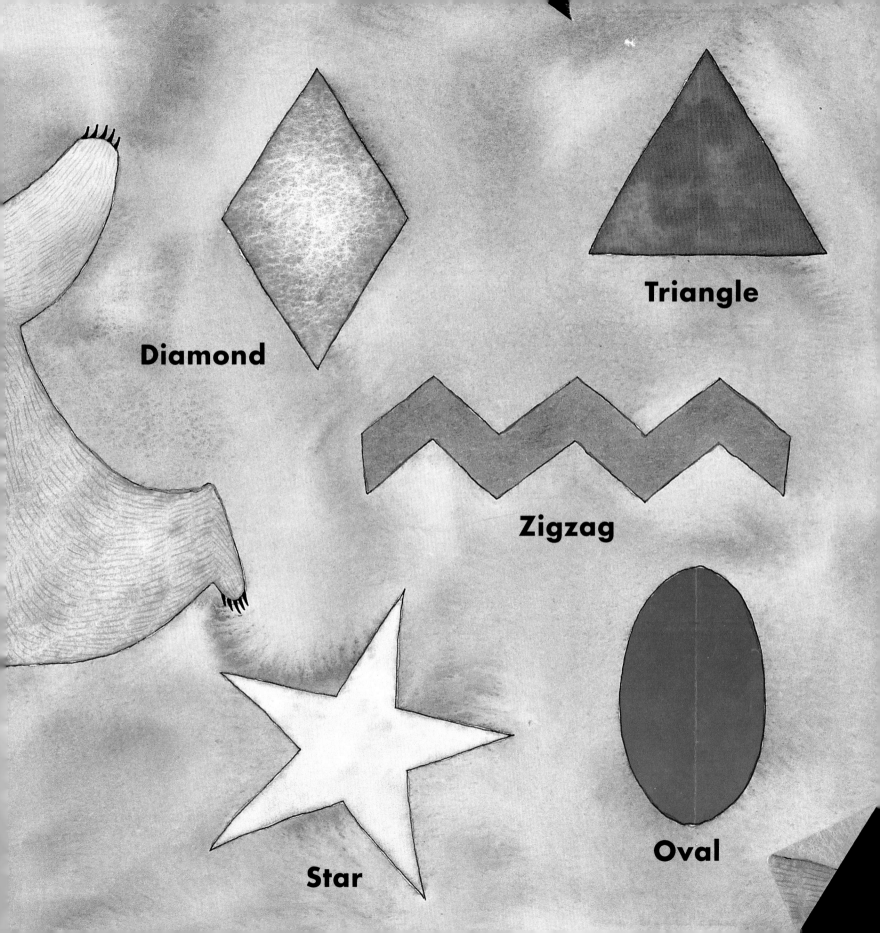

Diamond

Triangle

Zigzag

Star

Oval

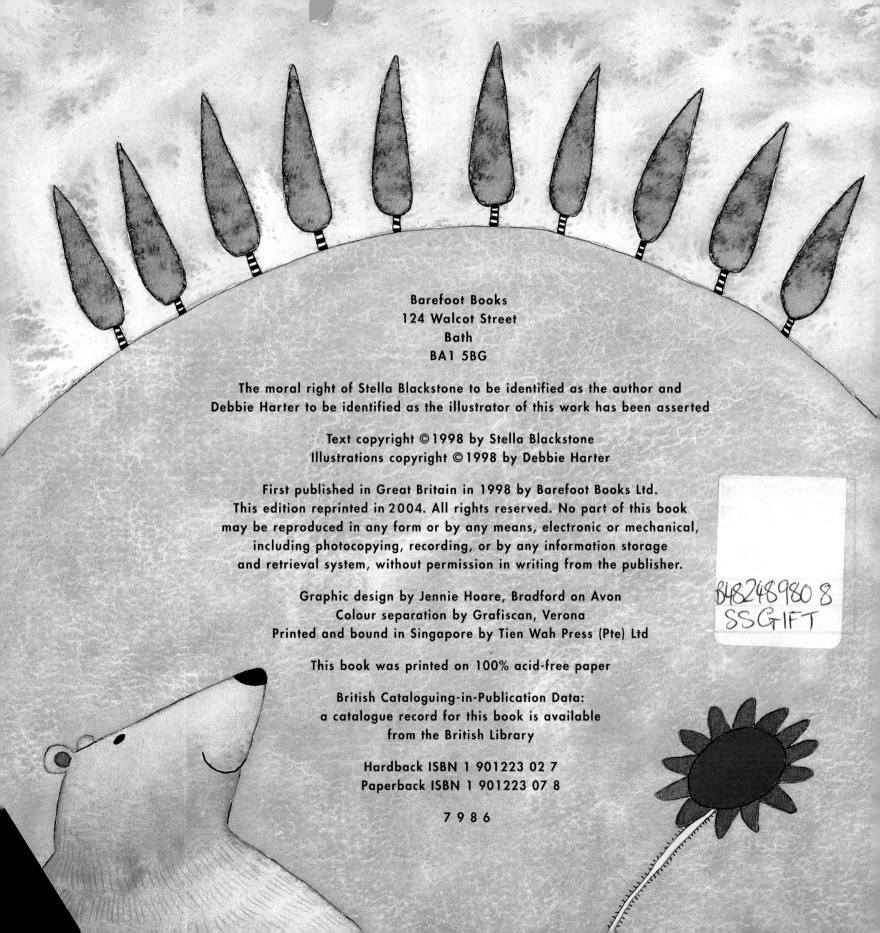

Barefoot Books
124 Walcot Street
Bath
BA1 5BG

Graphic design by Jennie Hoare, Bradford on Avon
Colour separation by Grafiscan, Verona
Printed and bound in Singapore by Tien Wah Press (Pte) Ltd

This book was printed on 100% acid-free paper

British Cataloguing-in-Publication Data:
a catalogue record for this book is available
from the British Library

Hardback ISBN 1 901223 02 7
Paperback ISBN 1 901223 07 8

7 9 8 6